Big Trouble on Bird Island

HarperFestival is an imprint of HarperCollins Publishers.

The Angry Birds™ Movie: Big Trouble on Bird Island
© 2016 Rovio Animation Ltd., Angry Birds, and all related properties, titles, logos, and characters are trademarks
of Rovio Entertainment Ltd. and Rovio Animation Ltd. and are used with permission. All rights reserved.
Printed in the United States of America.
No part of this book may be used or reproduced in any manner whatsoever without written permission except
in the case of brief quotations embodied in critical articles and reviews. For information address HarperCollins
Children's Books, a division of HarperCollins Publishers, 195 Broadway, New York, NY 10007.
www.harpercollinschildrens.com

ISBN 978-0-06-245340-2

16 17 18 19 20   CWM   10 9 8 7 6 5 4 3 2
❖
First Edition

THE ANGRY BIRDS™ MOVIE

BIG TROUBLE ON BIRD ISLAND

Illustrations by Tuğrul Karacan
Based on a story written by Sarah Stephens

HARPER FESTIVAL
An Imprint of HarperCollinsPublishers

It was a dark day on the usually cheerful Bird Island. Finch, a reporter at the *Daily Peep*, had the scoop on something bad that had happened downtown. If she wanted to make headlines, she needed to get moving.

Finch pushed her way through the crowd gathered in the town square. She was shocked. Somebody had pummeled the statue of Mighty Eagle, Bird Island's beloved hero, with rocks!

Finch listened to the birds' chatter. One name seemed to be on the tip of every beak: Red. She wrote it in her reporter's notebook.

Next Finch looked for clues. She saw a calm white bird with pink feathers step in front of the upset flock. It was Matilda, who ran the Infinity Acceptance Center.

"Everybody . . . take a deep breath," Matilda said.

The birds breathed in.

"Now let it go!" she continued.

The birds breathed out.

Finch followed along. She relaxed. It helped her focus on the case.

The next morning, Finch found out that the statue had been attacked again! Someone had splattered it with red paint.

Once more, Finch wrote *Red* in her notebook.

Matilda was back to calm the birds. "We'll start with some deep breaths and then do yoga," she said.

Finch wasn't at yoga, but she felt calm, cool, and ready to search for an angry red bird.

Finch found one at the beach. He was big. He was red. And he had a big frown because a little purple bird had kicked his sand sculpture.

"It was an accident!" the purple bird explained. "I tripped and fell into Terence's sculpture of Mighty Eagle!"

Finch took a closer look. "You were making a sculpture of Mighty Eagle?" she asked.

Terence nodded sadly. This bird was not the culprit.

Finch returned to the scene of the crime. She stared at the statue. What clue was she missing?

Finch noticed Matilda—still helping the crowd. She was teaching them to paint.

"Painting helps relieve stress," she said.

The small splotch of red paint on Matilda's feathers reminded Finch that she still had not found her one and only suspect: Red.

Just then, Finch spotted a bigger red splotch in the distance. It turned out to be an angry red bird, and he was headed her way!

"Is your name Red?" she asked.

"Yes," Red sputtered.

Finch asked him where he'd been the past two nights.

"I was home—sleeping! If I don't get enough sleep, I lose my temper. You would NOT want to see that."

Finch let Red go. She *definitely* did not want to see that.

Red's alibi was pretty flimsy. He lived alone. No one could back up his story. So Finch kept him on her list. She just needed to catch him red-handed.

When the sun set, Finch snuck down to the statue. She found a perfect spot. She coul see everything, but no one could see her.

The sky grew dark; the moon rose;
and Finch yawned. She was about to give
up hope when she heard a strange noise

Finch saw a spooky shape heading straight for the statue!
She held up her camera and began snapping shots just as the
figure began throwing toilet paper over Mighty Eagle's statue!

Finch uncovered the vandal, but it wasn't Red. It was Matilda, and she was sleepwalking!

"Wake up!" Finch yelled.

Matilda blinked and looked around. She spotted the statue covered in toilet paper and dropped the rolls she was holding.

"Oh no!" said Matilda.

"Oh yes," Finch said, nodding.

The next day, Matilda appeared in court.

"I used to be a very angry bird," she said. "I controlled my anger with meditation and yoga. I was cured. But I guess there's a little bit of anger nesting inside me, and it wakes up when I'm asleep!"

The judge sentenced her to one hundred hours of community service cleaning up Bird Village—starting with the statue of Mighty Eagle.

Finally, Finch cracked the case and broke her first big story.

BIRD

DAILY PEEP

SLEEP-
WALKING
NIGHTMARE

ANGER MANAGER
NEEDS MANAGEMENT